Me and My Cat?

Fife Council Education Department

King's Road Primary School

King's Crescent, Rosyth KY11 2RS

Late one night an old lady in a pointed hat came in through the bedroom window. She brandished her broom at me and fired out some words. Then she left without saying goodbye . . .

A Red Fox Book

Published by Random House Children's Books
20 Vauxhall Bridge Road, London SW1V 2SA

A division of The Random House Group Ltd
London Melbourne Sydney Auckland
Johannesburg and agencies throughout the world

Copyright © Satoshi Kitamura 1999

1 3 5 7 9 10 8 6 4 2

First published in Great Britain by Andersen Press Limited 1999

Red Fox edition 2001

Printed in Hong Kong

THE RANDOM HOUSE GROUP Limited Reg. No. 954009

www.randomhouse.co.uk

ISBN 0 09 942307 3

Me and My Cat?

SATOSHI KITAMURA

"Nicholas, wake up! You'll be late for school."
It must be Mum. It must be morning again.

Mum dragged me to the bathroom and made me
wash and dress.

Downstairs she interrupted my breakfast.
She was furious.
She carried me off to catch the school bus.
I had gone . . .

but I was still here . . .

"How strange," I thought to myself, pulling my whiskers.

WHISKERS?!

I rushed to the bathroom and looked at myself
in the mirror. Leonardo, my cat, was staring back at me.
But it wasn't him. It was me!
I couldn't believe my eyes.
I had turned into a cat!

"Don't panic," I told myself.
I sat in the armchair to consider the situation
carefully . . .
I fell asleep.

When I woke up, I felt a little better.
Maybe it wasn't such a bad thing to be a cat.
I didn't have to go to school, did I?
I hopped onto the table, and from there to the top
of the shelf.
What fun! I could never do *this* before.

I made a leap towards the cupboard on the other side of
the room . . .

OOPS!

Mum threw me out of the house.

While I was rambling in the garden, Gioconda,
the next-door cat, came up and licked me all over my face.
Yuck!
"Time to go for a walk," I thought.

The brick wall was warm under my paws.

When I came to Miss Thomson's garden I saw Heloise.
A strange feeling came over me.

Miss Thomson had given me Leonardo as a kitten.
Leonardo was Heloise's son.
Did that mean *she* was now my mother?
"Miaow, Miam (Hello, Mum)," I called tentatively.
She ignored me completely.

Further along I came across three mean-looking cats.
"Excuse me. May I go through?" I said.
"No, go away! It's our wall," replied one.
"I think the wall belongs to every . . ."
But before I could finish my sentence
they were all over me.

We punched and kicked and scratched one another
until we fell off the wall, entangled.
"Bowwowowowowowowowow!"
A dog came running towards us, barking furiously.
The cats ran away in all directions.
It was Bernard, Mr Stone's dog.
He's a sweet dog, my favourite
in the neighbourhood.

"Thanks, Bernard. You came just in time . . ."
But he chased me out of the garden.
Of course! He couldn't recognise me.

So this was the world that Leonardo lived in.
Life was as tough and complicated as it was for humans.

When I got home, I heard a strange noise coming from
the front door.

It was "me" back from school, trying to get into the house through the cat flap.
But was he me, Nicholas? Or, was he poor little Leonardo inside my body?

Once inside, he continued to behave strangely.
He scratched himself earnestly and when that was done
he challenged his shoes until they surrendered.

He licked his jumper clean, then spent a long time sharpening his nails.
He found the goldfish particularly fascinating.

He tried to sort the washing, and the wool . . .
but at last he gave up.

He thought the radiator irresistible and was potty about the cat's toilet.

But when he noticed *me* he didn't seem to like my face at all.

Mum saw something was wrong with her son, at last.
She became so worried that she called the doctor and asked
him to come at once.

"Nothing to worry about," said Doctor Wire. "He's just a little over-tired. Send him to bed early and he'll be fine in the morning."

Mum was still very upset. She held him tight in her arms
all evening. I felt sorry for them both.
I climbed on Leonardo-in-my-shape and stroked his cheek.
He purred. Then, Mum stroked me gently. I purred.

Later that night the old lady in the pointed hat came in
through the bedroom window.

"Sorry, love. I got the wrong address," she said.

She brandished her broom and blurted out some words.

Then, she left without saying good night.

"Nicholas, wake up! You'll be late for school,"
I heard Mum shouting.
Everything was back to normal.

At school Mr McGough sat on the table.
He scratched himself, licked his shirt
and fell asleep for the rest of the lesson.

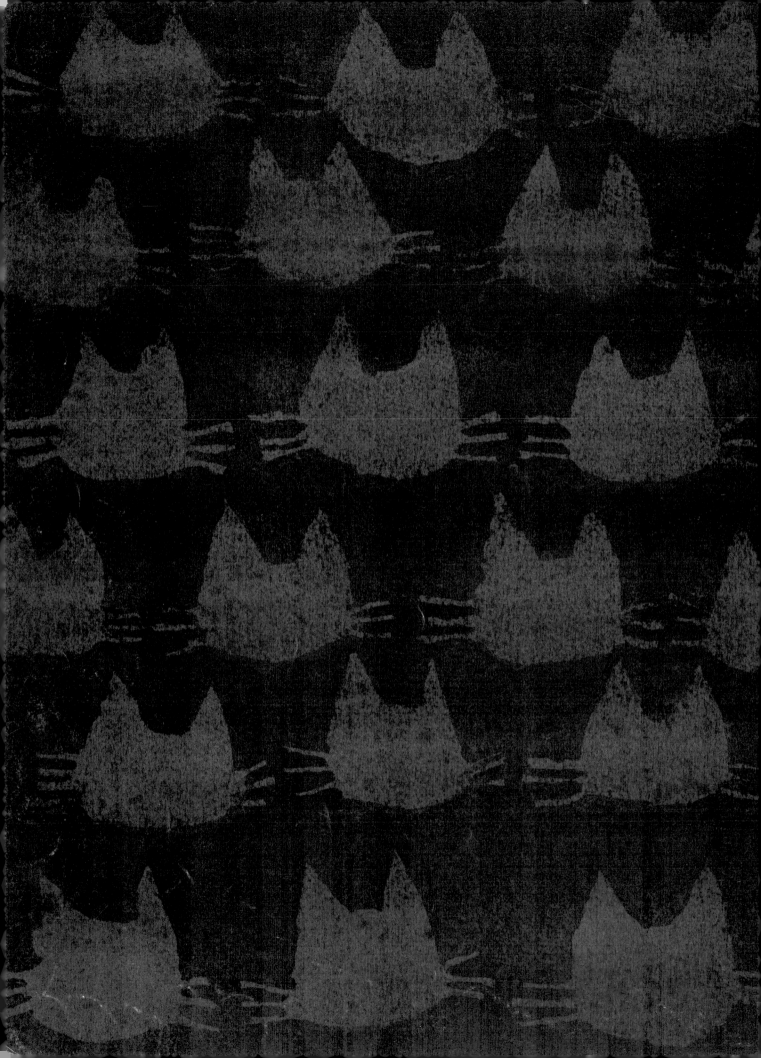